The Secret Mermaid

Enchanted Shell

Sue Mongredien

Illustrated by Maria Pearson

USBORNE

For Hannah Powell,
who helped with lots of good ideas for this story.

First published in the UK in 2009 by Usborne Publishing Ltd., Usborne House,
83-85 Saffron Hill, London EC1N 8RT, England. www.usborne.com

Copyright © Sue Mongredien Ltd., 2009
Illustrations copyright © Usborne Publishing Ltd., 2009

A CIP catalogue record for this book is available from the British Library.
This edition published in America in 2016 AE.
PB ISBN 9780794534868   ALB ISBN 9781601303714
JFMAMJJ SOND/17 01523-13
Printed in China.

Contents

The Mermaids of the

Molly

Ella

Delphi

Shivana

Undersea Kingdom

Coral

Queen Luna

Princess
Silva

Pearl

Chapter One

Molly Holmes raced across the deserted
beach as fast as she could. The sand was cool
and damp beneath her bare toes, and the
waves were white curls of foam on the
shoreline. Seagulls screeched overhead, and
Molly laughed out loud. This was her beach
now. Her beach!

She slowed to a jog, smiling. It had seemed
like a bad dream when her mom and dad had

first told her that they would all be moving, to live with Molly's gran.

Gran had had a bad fall, and Molly's parents had decided they wanted to be with her, now that she was getting older. Molly loved her gran, but still hadn't wanted to move away from her friends and school.

"Horseshoe Bay is miles from Katie and my other friends," she'd protested. "I'll never get to see them!"

Her mom had hugged her tightly. "We've got the whole summer to settle in, and for you to make friends before school starts," she'd said. "And you and Katie can call each other – and she can come and stay sometimes."

Molly hadn't felt reassured, though. She didn't want to move, simple as that! There was no way she'd ever make a friend who was even half as much fun as Katie. And she'd hated seeing her cozy little bedroom all bare, with everything packed up in boxes. "Can't Gran come and live with us here?" she'd asked. "She could have the spare room."

Her mom had shaken her head. "It's not as simple as that, Molly," she'd replied. "And besides, your dad and I think it'll be fun to live by the sea. I'm sure you'll love it when you've settled in."

"I'm sure I *won't* love it," Molly had muttered to herself in bed last night. "I know I won't!"

Molly scooped up a handful of sand, and let the wind blow it between her fingers. Now that they were actually here at The Boathouse, she felt differently.

She hadn't been to Gran's house for almost a whole year, after all. She'd forgotten the big garden with its twisty apple trees and a swing that hung from an old oak. She'd forgotten the way the kitchen at The Boathouse always smelled of baking. She'd forgotten how wonderful Gran was at telling stories, too, curled up with Molly in the saggy green armchair. Best of all, she'd been given the attic bedroom to sleep in!

Molly grinned. The bedroom in her old house had looked over their street. It had been noisy in the morning, with people slamming their front doors and driving off to work. But her new bedroom... Well! It was about as perfect as you could get. It was all white, with sloping ceilings and a funny little window that looked out onto the beach.

The house was so near the bay that Molly could hear the waves crashing on the shore and smell the salty air whenever the window was open. And oh, she just loved the beach already!

Molly sat on the sand, hugging her knees to her chest as she gazed around. Horseshoe Bay was a small cove, with huge rocks around its curving sides, and soft, golden sand. It was so pretty!

So maybe – just maybe – living here was going to be all right... As long as she could make a new friend to play with, of course.

"Molly! Let's go in now – it's time for some food!"

Molly looked over to where her mom was standing, with Molly's baby brother Toby, at the far end of the cove. Suddenly she was starving. She jumped up and raced across the sand toward them. "Coming!" she yelled.

Molly's dad had helped Gran set out some food on the old wooden picnic table in the backyard. There were crusty rolls with butter and crab paste, and a dish of cucumbers and cherry tomatoes. It was fun sitting out there, listening to the seagulls shriek and the waves thundering in down below on the beach.

Molly ate two rolls, then a huge slab of cherry cake, and gave a big yawn.

Gran smiled. "That'll be the sea air," she said knowingly.

"I think someone needs an early night," Molly's mom said, sliding an arm around Molly's shoulders and giving her a squeeze. "It's been a long day."

"You'll have sweet dreams up in that attic room," Gran assured her. "That was always my bedroom when I was a girl, you know. And your father slept there too, when he was a boy."

"It's true," Molly's dad said. "And the racket those seagulls used to make every morning – I didn't miss them when I left home, believe me!"

Gran winked at Molly. "Don't listen to him," she said. "You'll get used to the gulls in no time." She leaned over the table toward Molly, lowering her voice. "You're going to love sleeping there. I just know it."

An hour or so later, Molly sat on the edge of her bed in her pajamas. She had to keep reminding herself that she lived here now, in Gran's house. Somehow it didn't seem real yet. She couldn't help thinking back to her old room, where she'd slept for so many years until today. It was weird to think about somebody else in there now.

"Sweet dreams," Gran had said, as Molly kissed her goodnight downstairs. "Oh, and Molly?" She put a hand in her apron pocket and pulled something out. "This is for you," she said.

Molly stared down at the necklace that Gran pressed into her hand. The chain was silver, with

a curving piece of shell attached to it. The shell fit perfectly into her palm, and was smooth and cold against her skin. One side was a creamy white, and the other was mother-of-pearl, gleaming green and pink as Molly turned it. "Thank you," Molly said in surprise. "But..."

"It's a piece of a conch shell," Gran said. "And it's very special."

"What happened to the rest of it?" Molly wanted to know.

Gran pulled her in for a last hug. "It was broken," she said vaguely, kissing the top of Molly's hair. "Now, I'd better help your mom and dad with the dishes, I think," she said, before Molly could ask any more questions. "Goodnight."

Up in her room, Molly crossed to the window and gazed out at the sea. The tide had come right into the bay now, and the water was tinged with scarlet streaks where the sun was starting to set.

"All ready for bed?" came her mom's voice just then.

Molly turned to see her parents in the doorway. "Look what Gran gave me," she said, holding up the necklace.

Her dad let out a whistle of surprise. "I remember that piece of shell!" he said. "It was always on our mantelpiece when I was a boy. Imagine her still having it, after all those years! Your gran never let me and your Uncle Harry play with it, Molls. Used to say it was too special for us boys to mess with!"

Her mom smiled. "She must trust you, then, Molly," she said, walking over to close the curtains. "Come on, into bed now. Why don't you leave the necklace on the bedside table – and then maybe you'll dream about the sea."

"I hope so," Molly said, pulling back her covers and sliding her legs underneath. She put the shell necklace next to her bedside lamp. "Night, Mom. Night, Dad," she added, lying back on her pillow.

Her mom and dad kissed her goodnight. "Sleep well," her mom said.

Molly lay awake in the darkness, as her parents pulled the bedroom door shut behind them. There was no way she was ever going to get to sleep tonight, she decided. There was far too much to think about for that!

She tossed and turned for a while, her mind

drifting in and out of thoughts. Then, as she rolled over for what seemed like the hundredth time, she caught sight of the shell necklace on her bedside table, and gasped.

A strange pinkish light was streaming from the curved shell, and the air around it was filled with tiny golden sparkles. Molly stared in surprise, then sat upright and rubbed her eyes. But when she took her hands away, everything was dark again.

Did I just imagine that? she wondered, groping around for the necklace. Her fingers curled around the shell and she picked it up. This time, it felt warm, as if it had been lying in the sun all day.

Molly frowned, trying to make sense of what she'd seen – or what she *thought* she'd just seen. *Was I asleep after all?* she wondered. *Was it just a dream? Because everyone knows that shells don't glow and sparkle like that! Not unless they're...*

She shivered with excitement. *Not unless they're magical!*

Chapter Two

Molly held the necklace for a few moments, but nothing else happened.

I must have imagined the whole thing, she thought, snuggling back under the blanket, the shell still in her fingers. *Maybe it was just the moon shining through a gap in my curtains... or a dream...*

She closed her eyes, too tired to think about it any longer, and fell fast asleep almost at once.

When Molly opened her eyes, she wasn't
sure where she was at first. Her bedroom
had vanished. She was...she was
underwater!

Molly stared around. The water was
warm and clear, and below her she could
see fronds of seaweed waving gently,
and brightly colored shells. A school of
azure-blue fish darted past her. But
where was she? How did she get here?

And why did her legs feel so very strange?

She gave them an experimental wiggle and found herself surging forward through the water. That didn't usually happen! She glanced over her shoulder, puzzled. And then she realized...

"I've got a tail!" she cried out. Her eyes widened in astonishment at the sight of her very own sparkling green-scaled tail flicking behind her.

"And I can talk underwater!" she laughed. Silver, wobbling bubbles floated out of her mouth with each word. She could hardly believe it was real. "And I'm a..." She gasped, as she realized what had happened. "I really am a..."

"You're a mermaid!" came a tinkling voice.

Molly twirled around to see another mermaid swimming toward her. She had bright golden hair, shoulder-length and wavy, with a pretty pink flower behind one ear. The top half of her looked just like a normal girl, wearing a pink and silver patterned top. But under her belly button, where her legs should have been, was a shimmering blue tail, swinging from side to side as she swam.

The smiling mermaid did a graceful somersault in the water. "I'm Ella," she said to Molly, her green eyes bright and friendly.

"I'm Molly," Molly replied in wonder, realizing that her pajamas had vanished, as well as her legs. She glanced down to see that she was wearing a turquoise top instead, and her shell necklace. "And I'm a mermaid!" she shouted joyfully, trying to do a somersault like Ella.

"Wow!" she cried, spinning through the warm water. "This is so much fun!"

Ella's eyes had gone very wide. She was staring at Molly with a shocked expression on her face. "Is that...is that...?" she stuttered, pointing a finger at Molly's necklace.

Molly was taken aback by Ella's expression and glanced down at the necklace. "This? It's a piece of conch shell," she told Ella. "My gran gave it—"

Ella looked dazed. "I know what it is," she said faintly before Molly could finish, and then a smile broke over her face and she flung her arms around Molly's neck. "So you're our new secret mermaid! Oh, this is so exciting!"

"What?" Molly asked in surprise, her face full of Ella's golden hair.

"Oh, welcome! Welcome!" Ella exclaimed. "Welcome to the Undersea Kingdom! We've been wondering when you would come. Olive used to visit all the time, but it's been ages since she last came."

"Olive?" Molly echoed. "But...that's my gran's name..."

"Yes, I know," Ella said, tugging at Molly's hand. "Come on!" she cried. "We're going to the Merqueen's palace. She'll be so delighted that you're here!"

"But..." Molly was struggling to make sense of all this. Surely Ella wasn't really trying to tell her that *Gran* had met the mermaids, too? "Wait, I—" she said, but Ella was already pulling her through the sea.

"Come on, Molly! I'll explain everything later, I promise!" she said.

Molly followed
Ella as she went
diving down
deeper and
deeper. Mermaid-
swimming was
really different
than ordinary
swimming, Molly
soon realized. Just
flicking her tail sent her
zooming forward at a great speed –
it was much easier than front crawl!

After they'd been swimming for a while,
Ella glanced back at Molly. "Almost there,"
she called. "See the gates ahead?"

Molly peered through the water to where
she could just see two golden gates rising up
from the bottom of the ocean.

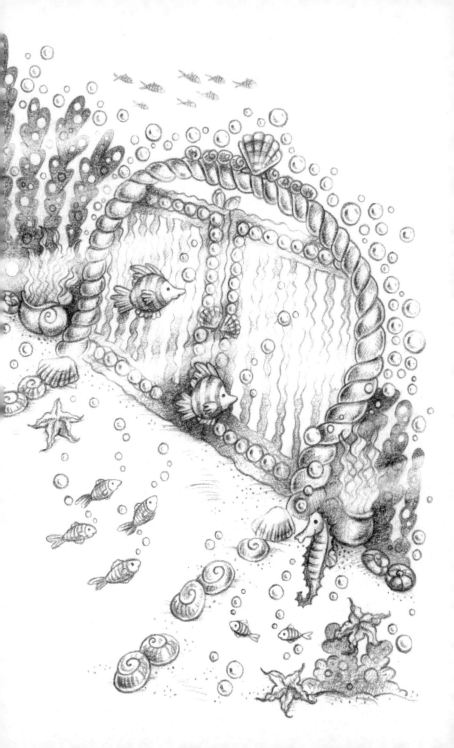

She felt a twist of excitement at the thought of meeting Ella's friends and the Merqueen on the other side.

 Ella pulled a small golden key out of a tiny bag that dangled from a chain around her wrist, unlocked the gates, and pushed them open. She slipped through, beckoning Molly to do the same...but just as Molly was about to follow, a huge black octopus with red glowing eyes appeared out of nowhere, shoving her roughly aside with one of its long rubbery tentacles, and dragging the gates shut with another.

"Hey!" Molly cried in fright. The octopus was wrapping a tentacle around her neck and she grabbed at it, trying to wrench it off. The tentacle was thick and strong though, and she couldn't move it at all.

Meanwhile, she could hear Ella rattling the
gates, trying to open them. "Get away!" Ella
shouted. "Leave her alone!"

But the octopus clung fast to the gates, keeping them firmly shut, as well as tightening its grip on Molly. With a jolt of horror, Molly realized it was trying to pull off her beautiful necklace, the one Gran had given her!

Molly felt a surge of anger. There was no way she was going to let her new necklace be taken from her!

"Oh no you don't!" she shouted, flailing within its grip and raining blows on its squishy head. The octopus didn't seem to notice, and, for the first time, Molly found herself wishing she still had her legs so that she could use them to kick out. She couldn't let it take her necklace! She couldn't! But what else could she do to stop it?

Chapter Three

In desperation, Molly gripped her conch shell,
trying to protect it from the octopus's reaching
tentacles and wishing the creature would leave
her alone. Just as the thought left her head,
the shell suddenly felt warm in her palm and
the water around her fingers shimmered pink.
She glanced down at the shell in surprise to see
that it was surrounded by a bright, glittery pink
light, just as it had been back in her bedroom.

The light from the shell streamed out toward the octopus and swirled around it. Then the octopus made a surprised hissing sound and Molly stared in disbelief as its tentacles became tangled up with one another until they were one big knot.

Writing and thrashing, it backed away clumsily, scrabbling to untie itself.

Meanwhile, Ella had yanked open the gates and dragged Molly through to the other side. "Oh, Molly!" she said. "Are you all right?"

Molly was panting and felt trembly with shock, but more than anything, she was relieved not to have lost her shell necklace. "I think so," she said, still holding onto it. The pink light was fading now, until, with a last few golden sparkles, it disappeared. "What...what happened?" she asked wonderingly. "Did my shell make the octopus get tangled up like that? And why was it attacking me, anyway?"

Ella locked the gates, her fingers shaking as she used the golden key. "I can't believe it," she said. "The Dark Queen must have sensed your piece of shell was here..." She frowned, lost in her thoughts, and Molly felt utterly confused.

"I don't understand," she said. "Who's the Dark Queen?"

Ella's face was grave. "A bad mermaid," she said simply. "But we're safe from her now that we're here. The Dark Queen's army can't come into our Kingdom – the boundaries are guarded by magic." She glanced through the gates, where the octopus was drifting away. "But if they know about the shell, we'd better tell Queen Luna – *our* queen – right away." She took Molly's hand. "And I can explain everything then, okay?"

Molly nodded and followed Ella, gazing around at the Kingdom.

There were clusters of what looked like small,
curving caves, built of white rock. They all
seemed to be decorated in a different
way, so that each was unique. One
had pink sea-flowers around the
windows, another had a roof
tiled with what looked like
orange coral, and a third
had glittering silvery shells
all around its doorway.

There were mermaids playing, swimming and talking everywhere that Molly looked, as well as the cutest little sea horses bobbing about, and great schools of colorful tropical fish streaming in all directions. And then, of course, there was the palace.

The mermaid palace was like no other building Molly had seen before. It was a far grander version of the caves – and, with its three white stories, Molly thought it looked like the most gorgeous, elaborate wedding cake ever made! Each story was intricately carved, with turrets and towers and balconies. It was like something out of a fairy tale.

"Queen Luna lives there, with Princess Silva,"
Ella said, her voice breaking into Molly's
thoughts. "See that heart-shaped window, right
at the top? That's Princess Silva's bedroom."

"Wow," Molly breathed, unable to take
her eyes off the magnificent building. "It's
beautiful!"

"Coral! Delphi!" Ella called just then,
waving to a couple of other mermaids.
"Over here!"

Molly saw a dark-haired mermaid and an
auburn-haired mermaid riding on two
friendly-looking dolphins nearby. They turned
and came over at Ella's shout.

"Want to join us? We're having races!" the dark-haired mermaid said. Her beautiful violet eyes were curious as she looked at Molly. "Hello, I'm Coral. Where have you come from?"

"Horseshoe Bay," Molly replied. "Although I'm not sure how I ended up here. My gran gave me a shell necklace, you see, and—"

"Look," Ella said, pointing at it.

Coral let out a gasp. Delphi clapped a hand to her mouth. "Is that what I think it is?" Delphi asked.

Ella nodded. "Yes," she replied. "And the Dark Queen has already tried to steal it from her. We're going to see Queen Luna right away. Will you come?"

"Of course," Coral said. She smiled at Molly. "I can't believe you're here!"

"We are so happy to see you," Delphi chimed in.

"Thank you," Molly said, "but I still don't really know—"

"Don't worry," Ella interrupted. "The queen will explain. Let's go to the palace and find her."

Chapter Four

Coral and Delphi slid away from their dolphins, and kissed their silvery noses goodbye, waving as the happy creatures gracefully raced away. Then the four mermaids swam up to the grand mother-of-pearl doors at the front of the palace. A pair of lobsters stood on guard before the doors, and clicked their long pincers at the mermaids as they approached.

"Who goes there?" one asked in a scratchy

kind of voice. Ella gave him a knowing look. "You know exactly who I am," she said. "And Coral and Delphi, too. But you don't know Molly. She's the new secret mermaid. And we're taking her to meet Queen Luna, of course!"

The lobsters turned their stalky eyes to gaze upon Molly in interest. Then they scuttled aside. "You may enter," they said.

Ella swam forward and pushed open the large gleaming doors, then led Molly by the hand into a great hall. The ceiling was high and curving, and inlaid with thousands of tiny sparkling jewels that sent their colorful reflections through the water in all directions. It felt to Molly as if she were in some kind of watery kaleidoscope.

At the far end of the hall, Molly could see two mermaids on golden thrones.

The older one was very elegant-looking, with a golden crown on her coiled chestnut hair. A diamond sparkled on a chain around her throat, and she wore a sheer, flowing cape of deepest blue around her shoulders. The younger mermaid wore a silvery crown on her head and a shimmering purple cape.

Ella took Molly's hand and led her toward the two regal-looking mermaids. "Your Majesties, this is Molly," Ella said politely.

"Molly, this is Queen Luna and her daughter, Princess Silva." Then a grin broke across her face, as if she couldn't contain her excitement any longer. "Queen Luna, look what Molly's wearing around her neck!"

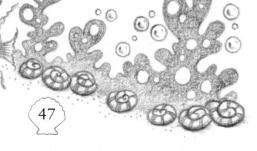

The Merqueen's eyes went very wide as she stared at Molly's necklace, and then she let out a cry of delight, and swam over to Molly. She clasped Molly's hands in her own, and smiled, her face alight with happiness. "Is it really true?" she asked, reaching out to gently finger the shell around Molly's neck. "Oh, but this is wonderful news!"

Molly felt nervous with the queen right there in front of her and wondered if she should curtsy, but wasn't quite sure how to, with a tail instead of legs. She bowed her head instead. "Hello," she said shyly.

"We have been waiting so long for our new secret mermaid to appear," the Merqueen went on, the words bubbling joyfully from her lips. "And now here you are, just at the right time!"

"Here I am," Molly echoed, "but please – I really don't understand. I don't know how I got here, or…"

The Merqueen smiled again and held up her hand to stop Molly. "I will explain everything," she said, "but let's go out to my private garden. We will be more comfortable there. Princess Silva, it's time for your lessons now. Off you go, my dear."

The princess was staring at Molly's shell necklace with a strange expression on her face, and didn't seem to hear her mother.

"Silva?" Queen Luna repeated. "Time for your lessons."

The princess jumped at the Merqueen's words and tossed her hair in a rather sulky way. "Okay," she muttered, and her eyes flicked one last time to Molly before she swam silently off.

Molly watched her go a little curiously –
the princess certainly wasn't as friendly as her
mother! – but then turned back to the
Merqueen to hear her giving one of her
servants an order. "Ask them to come right
away," she was saying.

Then Queen Luna led the way through the palace, and into a little courtyard garden, where jade green fronds of seaweed drifted gently in the current. She showed Molly and the others to large rocks, covered with soft velvety sea moss, where they could sit, and settled herself in an enormous pink scallop shell.

"Let me explain," she said to Molly. "You look as if you are bursting with questions."

Molly smiled. "I am," she admitted.

The Merqueen folded her hands in her lap and began. "Long ago," she said, "there lived the greatest mermaid of all. Her name was Lyria. And Lyria had a conch shell that could work strong magic, which she used to help any mermaid or human that needed it. In fact, it was powerful enough to keep all of the oceans and seas balanced and harmonious. But Lyria's sister, Elsina, was jealous of the conch. She wanted to use it for herself, to make herself the most important mermaid in the ocean. And when Lyria refused to give it to her, Elsina smashed it into pieces."

Molly's fingers crept around her shell pendant as she listened.

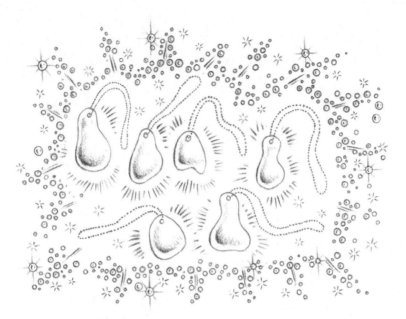

"Lyria found the pieces – six in all," the queen went on, "and the magic was still as powerful as ever, when she fit them back together. But Lyria was worried that Elsina would try to steal the shell, so she gave a single piece to each of her six daughters to look after."

The queen paused for breath, her green eyes upon Molly. "The six sisters grew up and went their different ways. They could each perform their own kind of magic to protect the areas of the ocean in which they lived, but whenever the six came together and used their shell pieces to make the conch whole, they could work the powerful magic again. They were known to everyone as the Shell-Keepers."

Molly found she was holding her breath, waiting to hear what came next. She could hardly believe that her gran was going to be part of this amazing story.

"The years went by and the six sisters passed the shell pieces down to their daughters, who then passed them down to *their* daughters," the queen went on. "But then the youngest daughter fell in love with a fisherman, and when she clambered out of the sea to be with him, she lost her tail and had legs in its place." The queen smiled at

Molly's surprised expression. "This daughter married the fisherman and lived with him on land. However, whenever her sisters needed her in order to make their powerful magic with the shell pieces, they would call to her in her dreams, and she could join them as a mermaid while she slept."

Molly's brain was ticking, trying to work out what this had to do with her. "So do you mean...?"

The queen nodded, as if she knew what Molly was about to ask. "She became known as a secret mermaid. And ever since then, her daughters and granddaughters have had special powers," she went on. "Mermaid powers." She smiled. "Although they lived on the land, the shell gave them the power to transform into mermaids. And so long as you keep your shell safe, you can visit us when you are asleep at night, as a mermaid, too. Just as your grandmother did before you."

Molly gasped. She could hardly take this in. It was incredible! She was actually descended from a magical line of mermaids, from Lyria, the greatest mermaid herself!

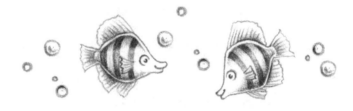

Chapter Five

Ella elbowed her. "And you'll never guess who three of the other descendants are," she said, with a wink.

Molly looked at her, then at Coral and Delphi, who had huge smiles on their faces. "You three?"

Coral nodded. "Yes," she said, "and there are two others as well, Shivana and Pearl. Shivana is our ice mermaid who takes care of the frozen wastes, and Pearl is the deep-water mermaid who looks after the very deepest parts of the ocean. You're sure to meet them soon."

"I have sent for them," Queen Luna said. "They should be with us in a few moments."

Molly turned to Ella, Coral and Delphi. "So where are *your* shell pieces, then?" she asked, excitement bubbling up inside her.

"Can we put them together, so that I can see—" She broke off at their disappointed expressions. "What? Have I said something wrong?"

"No," Delphi said sadly. "You haven't said anything wrong. It's just that..."

"We don't have them any more," Ella said, with a sigh.

The queen explained. "Although Elsina died long ago, her clan of Dark Mermaids live on," she said quietly. "Recently the five other shell pieces have disappeared – and we think they've been stolen by the current Dark Queen, Carlotta, and her army. We don't know how they've managed to breach the magic protection that surrounds our Kingdom, but somehow the conch pieces have vanished, one by one. And since they've been missing, terrible things have been happening at sea."

"Shipwrecks," Delphi put in. "There have been three since my piece of shell was taken. I am responsible for looking after sailors at sea and can usually protect them from storms, but it's very difficult without my shell."

"And I'm worried about the reef," Coral added, her eyes anxious. "Parts of it are already dying – because I don't have my shell to take care of it."

"The whole ocean is at risk while the Dark Queen has the conch pieces," Queen Luna said unhappily. "And there is only one piece left that she doesn't have."

Molly clutched at her necklace. "Mine?"

The queen nodded. "Olive has kept it safe for us for many years now, and you must do the same," she warned. "If the Dark Queen gets her hands on it..." She broke off and shuddered. "It would be a disaster," she finished quietly. "My guess is that she is plotting something that could destroy our whole Kingdom."

"She has already tried to steal Molly's shell," Ella put in. "We were attacked outside the city gates by one of her army – an octopus – but Molly managed to send it away, using her shell's powers."

Queen Luna looked shocked. "This is dreadful news!" she cried. Then she took Molly's hand in her own. "But you did well, my dear."

Molly glowed with pride at the queen's words, even though she wasn't quite sure how she'd set off her shell's magic. "I'll look after my piece of conch shell," she told the queen. "Of course I will! But what about the other pieces? Can't we try to get them back?"

Before anyone could answer, they heard a cry from outside the palace. "Let us in! We're here to see the queen!"

"It's Shivana!" Coral said.

Queen Luna swam out of the garden and returned moments later with two other mermaids. One had fiery red hair that fell in ringlets down her back and the other had dark brown pigtails, tied in green ribbons.

The red-haired mermaid came straight over to Molly. "I'm Shivana. Nice to meet you," she said in a businesslike way.

"And I'm Pearl," said the second mermaid, with a dreamy smile. "Hello."

"Hi," said Molly, feeling rather shy under Shivana's direct gaze.

"Now that we're all here, I think the best thing is to see what's happening in the Dark Queen's cave," the queen said. She went over to a large white rock, which looked as round and smooth as a giant marble. "This is the Seeing Stone," she explained to Molly. "With it, we can see into Carlotta's cave." Then she pressed both hands on its surface and shut her eyes for a moment.

Molly jumped in surprise as a picture appeared on the surface of the rock. The other mermaids crowded around to see, and she got up too and swam over, eager to know what they were looking at.

The picture on the rock showed a dark, gloomy cave, lined with shelves. "There it is!" Ella yelped suddenly, pointing. "The conch! Look – Carlotta has put the pieces together!"

Molly saw a huge, creamy-white shell on one of the cave shelves. She could see a slice missing from it – her piece, she knew, her heart pounding.

A mermaid with a mass of black hair and a hooked nose swam across the cave toward the conch. She wore a black, flowing cape around her shoulders, and a spiky silver crown on her head. "That's the Dark Queen, Carlotta," Coral whispered to Molly.

Molly shivered as the Dark Queen picked up the conch and held it lovingly. "Just one more piece to get," she crooned, "and then I will be able to—"

The conch shimmered with a golden light in the Dark Queen's hands and she stared at it. "What's happening?" she cried. "Why—?"

There was a loud cracking sound and suddenly the conch began to break apart.

"Stop!" the Dark Queen commanded.

"What is this magic? Stop, I tell you!"

"Wow," Pearl breathed, staring at the scene.

"Why is it doing that?"

Nobody replied. Instead, they all watched the Seeing Stone as it showed the pieces of the conch spiraling up away from the Dark Queen. Then the shell pieces vanished from sight, leaving the Dark Queen in a frenzy of rage. "Where have they gone?" she shrieked furiously. "Where have they *gone*?"

Chapter Six

There was a shocked silence among the mermaids. The picture vanished from the rock, and they all stared at one another.

"What happened?" Molly asked.

The Merqueen frowned, deep in thought. After a moment, she said, "I wonder if the conch broke apart with Molly's arrival in our Kingdom? It wouldn't surprise me. The conch has special powers of its own that we can't always predict."

Pearl nodded. "I think you're right," she said. "The return of the sixth piece gave a surge of power to the other five, perhaps."

"But where are our pieces? What's happened to them?" Coral asked.

Nobody seemed to have an answer. Just then, Molly heard a faint scraping sound behind her, and turned around anxiously. She'd felt on edge ever since the octopus had attacked her – but there didn't seem to be anything behind her now.

Shivana's eyes glittered. "Well, the Dark Queen seemed pretty furious – so I'm guessing they're not in her cave any more," she said. "Which means we might be able to find them again!"

The queen nodded. "We will all have to look," she said, a determined expression on her face. "We must find them before the Dark Queen's army does!"

Ella looked around. "Are we all in agreement? Molly? You too?"

Molly nodded, her fingers clasped around her own shell. "Yes," she said, feeling a fluttering sensation inside. She could hardly believe this was happening. "Yes, of course. I'll do anything to help."

The strange sound came from behind her again – and this time, when Molly turned around, she was sure she saw a shadowy figure darting out of sight. Or was it just the seaweed moving that she'd seen?

She turned back, realizing the queen was addressing her. "We'd love you to help, Molly," she was saying. "And the magic of your shell will assist you, once you know how to use it. But you must promise not to breathe a word of this to anyone in the human world, not even to your grandmother. Other humans will cause problems for us if they hear about our Kingdom and want to get involved. You are a secret mermaid. You must stay secret. Otherwise you will not be allowed into our Kingdom any more. Do you understand?"

Molly nodded, but inside she felt a huge wave of disappointment. She'd been looking forward to talking to Gran about the mermaids, and asking her about her own mermaid adventures, back when she was a girl. But she knew being able to come back to the Kingdom as a mermaid again and help find the missing conch pieces was more important. "I understand," she said solemnly.

The queen smiled at her. "Thank you," she said. "This must all be a shock for you, my dear – mermaids, octopuses and enchanted shells – but you have done well for your first time here. And I will send for you again very soon to help with our search."

Molly blinked. "You mean...? Aren't we going to go now? I thought..."

The Merqueen shook her head, and pointed to a shaft of light that had fallen across the garden. "It is time for you to leave us, I'm afraid, Molly," she said. "Dawn is on the way. It is almost time for you to wake up."

Molly bit her lip. She didn't want to leave the mermaids. Not yet! "But when...when will I see you again?" she asked. "When can I come back?"

The Merqueen put an arm around her shoulders. "I will send for you very soon," she repeated. "Until then... Farewell!"

Molly just had time to say goodbye to all of her new friends before she felt as if she was being hauled up to the surface of the ocean, rushing up through the water at great speed, with everything blurring before her.

"Molly! Breakfast's ready!"

Molly opened her eyes, her heart thumping. But...where was the sea? Where were Ella and the queen? Her head whirled as she tried to make sense of everything – and then she sighed. She was in her bedroom. It must have been a dream! The whole fantastical adventure was nothing but a dream. And yet it had seemed so real!

Molly sat up in bed, feeling disappointed. Her gaze fell upon the shell necklace which was lying on her pillow, and she picked it up and examined it. It was just a shell. Of course it was just a shell. How silly she was to think it was magical!

"Breakfast, Molly!" her mom shouted again. "It's on the table!"

"Coming, Mom!" she called, pulling on her bathrobe.

She opened the curtains, and there was the sea, retreating back from the beach now, its waves rolling and churning rhythmically. *Sssshhhh... Ssshhhh...* they seemed to be saying. Molly stared at the sea for a few moments, and, as she did so, she was sure she heard a faint, silvery voice calling her name.

Molly...

Molly...

"You're imagining it," she told herself, turning away from the window to go downstairs.

Sssssshhhh... Sssshhhhh... went the waves – and then the voice stopped.

Frowning, Molly clattered down to the kitchen, where her mom was cutting Toby's toast into strips. "There you are," her mom said.

"Sit down while your toast's still hot."
Her eyes grew wide as she looked at Molly.
"What *have* you got in your
hair? Is that seaweed?"

Molly put a hand
up to her hair
and felt a strip of
something soft
and cool at one
side. She picked it
off and looked at it.
It *was* seaweed!

"Where did *that* come from?" her mom
asked. "I didn't notice it when you went to
bed last night." She laughed. "Don't tell me
– you were out for a midnight swim," she
joked, turning back to Toby's toast.

Molly gazed at the green strand of seaweed
in her palm. "Weird," she managed to say,

despite her mom's words ringing in her ears. *Don't tell me – you were out for a midnight swim...*

Did it mean...? Had she *really* been swimming with the mermaids last night?

"Sit down, then, come on," her mom said. "Your toast will be stone cold at this rate, Molls!"

Molly slid into her chair and bit into the buttery toast, thinking hard. She couldn't really have met Ella and gone to the Undersea Kingdom, could she?

Her gran came into the kitchen just then, her eyes bright as a bird's. "Morning, Molly," she said, a little smile twisting her mouth. "Did you sleep well in your new bedroom?"

Molly stared at her gran and as she did so, her gran gave her a wink. Molly felt a jolt of excitement go through her. Gran *knew*.

She knew what had happened. Which meant... Molly could hardly believe it. So it *was* all true!

"Answer your gran, Molly," her mom said, glancing sideways at her. "Honestly, Olive, I don't know what's gotten into her this morning. She seems to have been struck speechless overnight, I think."

"Sorry," Molly mumbled. "I slept...fine, thank you, Gran. I..."

Her gran narrowed her eyes slightly and Molly stopped talking. She wasn't allowed to tell anyone about the mermaids. *Not even your grandmother,* the Merqueen had said. She ate another mouthful of toast, feeling churned up inside with wanting to talk about what had happened, but knowing she mustn't.

Gran sat down next to her and put an arm around Molly's shoulders. "I'm so glad you're all living here with me now," she said. "I think we're all going to have a very special time together in Horseshoe Bay. Don't you, Molly?"

Molly turned to look into Gran's lined, weathered face and smiled. To think she'd ever been worrying about moving here! Last night, she'd become a secret mermaid and visited the Undersea Kingdom. *And* she'd agreed to help her new mermaid friends find the missing pieces of the magical conch shell! "Yes," she replied to her gran, feeling a rush of happiness. "I think I'm going to love living here in Horseshoe Bay." She bit into her toast and smiled to herself. *And I can't wait to see the mermaids again soon!* she thought.

The End

For more magical
underwater adventures visit
www.edcpub.com
or
www.usbornebooksandmore.com

To find out more
about Molly and all her
mermaid friends, and have
some magical ocean fun,
check out

www.secret-mermaid.com

Sue Mongredien has published over 60 books, including the magical *Oliver Moon, Junior Wizard* series. Like Molly Holmes, Sue loves exploring, and gave up a job as an editor of children's books to travel the world, before becoming a full-time writer. Sue also loves the sea, and had a house near Brighton beach in England before moving to Bath, also in England, where she now lives with her husband and three children.

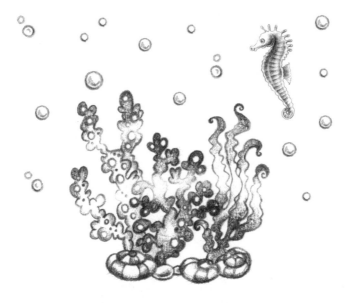

If you've enjoyed **The Secret Mermaid,**
you might also enjoy:

Amy Wild, Animal Talker

by Diana Kimpton

Welcome to the world of Amy Wild, where
dogs tell their secrets, cats perform rescue
missions, and an entire island is squeaking
and squawking with animal magic!

Animal lovers everywhere will be
instantly enchanted by this Dr. Dolittle
for a new generation.

The Pony-Crazed Princess

by Diana Kimpton

Princess Ellie is crazy about horses!
And she's fed up with being a princess!
She hates frilly pink dresses, and boring
waving lessons. She'd much rather be
riding one of her four gorgeous ponies!

SUNDANCE

RAINBOW

SHADOW

MOONBEAM